Bank Street

ABOUT THE BANK STREET READY-TO-READ SERIES

More than seventy-five years of educational research, innovative teaching, and quality publishing have earned The Bank Street College of Education its reputation as America's most trusted name in early childhood education.

Because no two children are exactly alike in their development, the Bank Street Ready-to-Read series is written on three levels to accommodate the individual stages of reading readiness of children ages three through eight.

○ *Level 1:* GETTING READY TO READ (Pre-K–Grade 1)
Level 1 books are perfect for reading aloud with children who are getting ready to read or just starting to read words or phrases. These books feature large type, repetition, and simple sentences.

○ *Level 2:* READING TOGETHER (Grades 1–3)
These books have slightly smaller type and longer sentences. They are ideal for children beginning to read by themselves who may need help.

○ *Level 3:* I CAN READ IT MYSELF (Grades 2–3)
These stories are just right for children who can read independently. They offer more complex and challenging stories and sentences.

All three levels of The Bank Street Ready-to-Read books make it easy to select the books most appropriate for your child's development and enable him or her to grow with the series step by step. The levels purposely overlap to reinforce skills and further encourage reading.

We feel that making reading fun is the single most important thing anyone can do to help children become good readers. We hope you will become part of Bank Street's long tradition of learning through sharing.

The Bank Street College of Education

For Mighty Mo
—S.A.

*To Rock who understands
the spirit of children*
—D.A.

MY WORST DAYS DIARY

A Bantam Book/September 1995

*Published by Bantam Doubleday Dell Books
for Young Readers, a division of Bantam
Doubleday Dell Publishing Group, Inc.
1540 Broadway, New York, New York 10036.*

Special thanks to Maggie Byer, Hope Innelli and Kathy Huck.

*The trademarks "Bantam Books" and the
portrayal of a rooster are registered
in the U.S. Patent and Trademark Office
and in other countries. Marca Registrada.*

Library of Congress Cataloging-in-Publication Data

*Altman Suzanne,
My worst days diary / by Suzanne Altman;
illustrated by Diane Allison
p. cm.—(A Bank Street ready-to-read)
"A Byron Preiss book."
Summary: Mighty Mo reveals in her diary
some of the most embarrassing moments
during her first year at a new school.
ISBN 0-553-09743-1 (hardcover)
ISBN 0-553-37575-X (trade paper)
[1. Schools—Fiction. 2 Moving,Household—Fiction.
3. Embarrassment—Fiction. 4. Diaries—Fiction.]
I. Allison, Diane, ill. II. Title. III. Series.
PZ7.A463954My 1994
[Fic]—dc20
94-37402 CIP AC*

Published simultaneously in the United States and Canada

PRINTED IN THE UNITED STATES OF AMERICA

0 9 8 7 6 5 4 3 2

TOP SECRET!!

MY (WORST DAYS DIARY

Name Maureen ("MO") Murphy

by Suzanne Altman
Illustrated by Diane Allison

A Byron Preiss Book

BANTAM BOOKS
NEW YORK • TORONTO • LONDON • SYDNEY • AUCKLAND

SEPTEMBER 5
Dear Worst Days Diary,
A trillion totally terrible disasters
keep happening to me.
So I'm starting this diary
to keep track of them all.
Here goes!
Today was the first—the WORST!—
day at my new school.

Our teacher said, "Stand up and
say your names very, VERY clearly."
When it was my turn, I took a deep breath
—and out came this humongous BURP!
"That is very rude," yelled Ms. Turro.
She thought I did it on purpose!
So did most of the kids in the class.
What a way to start!

J 45061

Dear Worst Days Diary,
In case you wonder what I look like:
My hair is the color of carrots and fire.
I have about forty million freckles.
My legs look like broomsticks with knees.
I'm the tallest kid in my class, so
I always stick out in a crowd.
Secret: I want to be a great actress—
a superstar of stage, screen, and TV!!!
I bet I can if I just try hard enough.
Yours truly,

Maureen Murphy

SEPTEMBER 15
Dear Worst Days Diary,
For homework we had to write
letters to our heroes.
I wrote, "Dear Katharine Hepburn,
You're the greatest star that ever lived."
I wrote all the reasons I admire her.
Then I wrote to Liz, my best friend
from my old school.

Guess which letter I handed in by mistake?
Guess which letter Ms. Turro read aloud?!?!
"Dear Liz, you're lucky you don't live here
or you'd be in Ms. Terror's class and
have to hear her YELL all the time."
There was a moment of awful quiet.
Then Ms. Turro roared, "See me at recess!"

When the class went out to play,
she gave me a big, long lecture.
"Don't you want to start out on
the right foot?" she asked me.
I nodded but didn't say a word.
Maybe I have two left feet.

Ms. Turro made me clean the chalkboards.
All the cool kids, <u>especially Amanda Nye</u>,
watched me through the window.

I made faces back at them,
and pretended I was a jazz dancer.

SEPTEMBER 23
Surprise—Amanda Nye
asked me to her birthday party!
I bought her a gift I hoped she'd like:
a neon jump rope that glows in the dark.
And I wore my coolest outfit.

I didn't want to be first at the party,
so I got there a little bit late.
Everything was real quiet.
I rang the bell . . . then rang it again.

No answer.
Nobody home?!?!
I thought, "Oh wow, really funny, Amanda.
You are so super-cool—I mean,
inviting me when there's no party."

I started to leave.
Then a car came up the driveway.
Amanda and her mom got out.
"Mo?" Amanda said, real surprised.
"Aren't you a little . . . early?"
I held out her gift
but she wouldn't take it.
"My party's *tomorrow*," she said.
"Think you can make it then?"
She and her mom went inside.
I thought I'd die.

I pretended to be invisible
and went slinking home.

I thought about going to the party
with a paper bag over my head.

Or I could change my name
and move to Zanzibar.

How will I face Amanda and her
cool friends tomorrow—or ever?

SEPTEMBER 24
Well, I went back.
I didn't even wear a paper bag on my head.
I expected to get teased out the door.
I was sure Amanda had told everyone
my stupid mistake . . .
especially her best friend, Cara.

But I don't think she did. . . .
Nobody even laughed at me till
my sunglasses fell into the frosting.

Then we all giggled—even me!

OCTOBER 5

Dear Worst Days Diary,
Today's a great day for ducks, but
yours truly should have stayed in bed.
It's raining cats and dogs.
There's gunk and muck everywhere.
When we trooped into class after lunch,
I thought my shoes were caked with mud.

During silent reading we all started
sniffing and gagging.
Yech! Gross! DOG DOO!

Kids started snickering.
I pretended to throw up and faint.

Ms. Turro pinched her nose and
pointed at my feet.
22   She turned a little green.

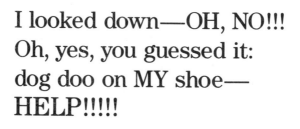

I looked down—OH, NO!!!
Oh, yes, you guessed it:
dog doo on MY shoe—
HELP!!!!!

j 45061

OCTOBER 18

Today were tryouts for the Halloween play.
The star is this spooky cat, Frowzle.
She has all the best lines
and steals every single scene.

EVERYBODY wanted to be that cat.
And guess who tried out really hard
... and GOT THE PART?!?!?

Yours truly, MIGHTY MO!

Hurray! MMMRRRROOOWWW!!!
Everybody clapped and cheered ...
EVEN MS. TURRO.
I guess it takes a superstar
to yell "MEOW!" like me!

OCTOBER 31: *HALLOWEEN*
The lights dimmed; the curtains parted.
Hundreds of kids held their breath.
THE HALLOWEEN PLAY BEGAN!

26

I, Frowzle the cat,
leaped onstage.
I swished my tail.
I bared my fangs.
I yowled a spine-chilling "MRRRROWWW!"

27

I could see all the kids sitting on
the edges of their seats.
I opened my mouth to say my first line.
But, BUT . . .
my mind went as blank as a turned-off TV.

I COULD NOT REMEMBER
ONE WORD!!!
"Cat got your tongue?"
called my big brother, Mike.
The whole audience cracked up.
Ms. Turro tried to help by
whispering my lines to me.
Goodbye, Hollywood.
Oh, Ms. Hepburn: forgive me!

NOVEMBER 13
Today I had a second chance to shine.
Ms. Turro invited me to act out my poem.
I pretended it was a screen test.

I stood up and smiled,
like for a real close-up shot.

I began, "To My Parakeet:
Is there a heaven in the sky,
For birds to fly to, when they die?"
I thought it was very sad and tragic,
but kids pointed and grinned like goons.

When I sat down, Cara gave me her mirror.
Yuck! This big, ugly, dark green
glob of spinach was stuck to my teeth.
P.S. I'll never smile again.

MARCH 21
Dear Diary, I lost you for
three whole months!
I found you in my costume trunk when I
got ready for Academy Awards night on TV.
I draped my strapless gown around me
and stepped into the spotlight.

I scooped up my hair, put on lipstick,
and smiled my most winning smile.
I clutched my Oscar to my chest
and started my speech:
"I want to thank my parents and—"

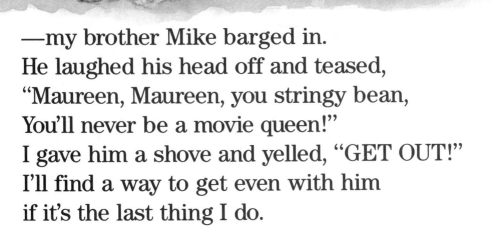

—my brother Mike barged in.
He laughed his head off and teased,
"Maureen, Maureen, you stringy bean,
You'll never be a movie queen!"
I gave him a shove and yelled, "GET OUT!"
I'll find a way to get even with him
if it's the last thing I do.

P.S. HA! I put pickle juice
in his deodorant.

APRIL 1
Dear Worst Days Diary,
Today I got to share my math project.
I worked on it all month.
Just before class, I ran to the girls' room
to check for stuff between my teeth.
I didn't want to go through THAT again!

I guess my shoe got kind of wet.
I didn't know the end of the toilet paper
got stuck on the bottom.

I didn't know it was dragging behind me
like a long white tail.

It unrolled behind me as I walked
out of the girls' room . . .

down the hall . . .
through the door . . .
and right to the front of my classroom.

Nobody heard a word I said.
They were too busy laughing.
Ms. Turro thinks I did it for April Fools'.
Does she think I'm NUTS?

APRIL 22
My Earth Day report started out great.
"I'm going to talk about a
close friend of the earth:
She's pretty as a ribbon.
She can curl up in a ball.
She hugs the ground when she moves,
and—"

Ms. Turro got curious and took off the lid.
"EEE-YIKES!!!"

She screamed so loud I dropped the box.
Hissy climbed out and slithered over
to where the cool kids sat.

"She's just a garter snake," I told them.
But they freaked out anyway.
It was a disaster!

APRIL 23
Dear Worst Days Diary,
I bet Cara and Amanda really
think I'm weird now—
because of my snake and all.
Each time the phone rings I think it's Cara,
dis-inviting me to her sleepover tomorrow.

APRIL 24

Cara didn't call, so off I went.
And the first thing she said was,
"Boy, Mo, are you brave!"

Then Amanda said, "We were hoping
you'd bring your snake so
we could get, uh, used to her."

So we went and got Hissy.
Everybody ended up thinking
she was really, really cool.

JUNE 18
School is almost over,
and it's ending on the right foot!
Dear Diary, can you believe
I have TWO best friends now?
Right, you guessed it—
Cara AND Amanda!

JUNE 21
Hello, Summer!
Goodbye, Ms. Terror!
What will you do without me?

Amanda, Cara, and I are going
to the same day camp.
On Pet Day we can bring our snakes.
And we'll all try out for the camp show.

JUNE 22

Dear Worst Days Diary,
I haven't had a WORST DAY in ages!
I don't even seem to have
BAD days these days.
So I'll put you away—
just in case I ever need you again.

Today I bought a brand-new notebook
with a bright, summer sky-blue cover.
I'll use it to write about all kinds of days—
especially my GREATEST DAYS!!!

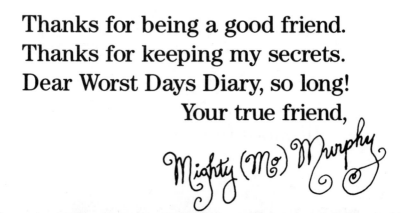

Thanks for being a good friend.
Thanks for keeping my secrets.
Dear Worst Days Diary, so long!
Your true friend,

Mighty (Mo) Murphy